# Futa Totem Collection #1

Danii Dezire

Published by Danii Dezire, 2015.

This is a work of fiction. Similarities to real people, places, or events are entirely coincidental.

FUTA TOTEM COLLECTION #1

**First edition. September 7, 2015.**

Copyright © 2015 Danii Dezire.

ISBN: 979-8201460747

Written by Danii Dezire.

Futa-Totem, Collection #1
by
Danii Dezire

# Copyright © 2014 by Danii Dezire

# Freaky Futa (Futa-Totem)

Sonia loved books almost as much as she loved sex. Almost.

Yet, she never thought the two would actually collide together until she met the cute new librarian.

Sonia had been going to that library for many years. Occasionally, there would be an attractive librarian working there. Usually, it was someone who primarily restocked shelves with the thousands of daily returns. The work itself required lots of kneeling, stretching and bending.

Many times Sonia envisioned hooking up with one of these sweethearts. So inspired by these fantasies, she even started to bring her magical Futa-Totem with her to the library, safely hidden in a satchel.

When one of these cuties worked in her area, she found that sitting in one of the lounge chairs gave Sonia a good view of their comings and goings. Desk cubicles, and their limiting view, where for the married, un-horny folk.

Sadly, though, there seemed to be a high turnaround at the library. Whether to internal library staff politics, general attrition (she couldn't imagine doing that type of work for years) or they here migrated to other branches, she never knew. But many hot, and/or cute, (or both) shelf re-stockers simply vanished from her almost weekly appreciations.

Or maybe they left because of her? Sonia had often wondered how obvious she was when she sneaked glances at their bums as the sauntered past, or bent down to add some books (That was certainly her favourite part of their job!). Each time, the Futa-Totem's wonderful use came to mind, too.

Also, as they were lost in the mundane concentration of their work, the almost never realized she was staring at their breasts. Side boob view was another favourite. You may not get a full appreciation of breasts full on, masked by a sweater or baggy blouse. But turned to the side, the breast was particularly arousing.

Then one day, there was a new little blond librarian. She was about Sonia's age, tiny in stature, but with a slim, yet very shapely figure. Thankfully, a lot of her books need restocking right in front of where Sonia was sitting.

Playing casual, Sonia peeked at her from over the edge of her book, thus allowing her to ogle the blonde's magnificent butt. *Jeans were created to be worn by this girl,* Sonia thought.

She had bent over, revealing the beautiful teardrop shape of her ass.

Sonia felt herself getting moist, and she looked down at her crotch, making sure everything was still in order and revealing anything too incriminatory.

"Found what you are looking for?" asked a pleasant female voice.

Sonia looked up, and blanched. It was her. The blond cutie standing directly in front of her.

*What did she mean? Looking for my wet spot? A book? Her?*

"Uh," was all Sonia could manage in that moment of shock. She became frighteningly aware of the wetness between her thighs.

*Did her eyes just flicker down at it?* Sonia thought, embarrassed. Maybe she was just looking at the book in her hand?

"Enjoying the selection?" the blond asked, with a crook of her eyebrow. Her expression seemed to show more than a passing interest in what Sonia's answer could be.

Was she flirting with her?

"Yeah, great selection. Thanks," Sonia said. *Geez, could I sound more stupid?*

"I'm Pam," she suddenly offered. "Just started here today."

Sonia was a little tongue tied, not expecting to have to actually *interact* with this object of desire. *Who'd of thunk of such a concept?*

"Sonia," she said. She found her heart was now thundering against her chest. Hopefully, her face didn't go red like it usually did when she was flustered.

"Well, Sonia," Pam said with a smile and a wink. "Maybe I'll see you around?"

"Yeah, definitely," Sonia said.

Pam turned to go, but paused. Sonia heart stopped.

She nodded her head at Sonia's... crotch? At her growing wetness? Sonia wanted to cross her legs but her erection would just make it look even funnier.

"By the way, you're reading it upside down," Pam grinned wickedly at her, and walked away, pushing the cart. Sonia could have sworn she put in an extra bit of sway to those perfect hips.

Sonia watched her leave, a bit in a daze. Looking at the book in her hands, she saw that Pam was right.

Stunned, Sonia waited for her dampness to subside. She even managed to read a little of the book (right side up this time), until she felt she had embarrassed herself enough for one day. She picked up her satchel, with its precious cargo, and decided to leave.

Sonia was walking towards the exit when she suddenly heard something.

"Sonia!" someone hissed from behind. She turned and was struck dumb when she saw that it was Pam. She was leaning around the end of a bookshelf, out of sight of the front door counter. She peeked down towards the counter then, looking back at Sonia, waved a hand at her, indicating she should come over.

Thankfully, Sonia's legs took the initiative and propelled her towards Pam, before her brain could screw things up.

When she got close, and obviously wasn't moving fast enough for her, Pam grabbed her arm and pulled her behind the shelves. Pam's firm touch electrified her bare skin. She found herself grinning.

Pam grinned back. "Got a question for you, Sonia." she said, looking quite beautiful.

"Okay," was all Sonia could say.

"Wanna fuck me?"

Sonia's breath caught.

*Oh.*

*My.*

*God.*

Her brain had seized up. Miraculously, she found herself nodding.

Pleased, Pam took her hand and quickly led her into a back room, which was filled with books, from top to bottom. Pam closed the door behind them.

"Are you up for some little fun, Sonia?" Pam asked.

*Duh.*

Shrugging, Sonia said, "Yeah, sure," she said, casually. Like getting propositioned by librarians was an everyday occurrence for her.

Pam nodded, but looked at her as if analyzing her honesty. "Not sure how much time I we have before closing. Was there something you had in mind?" she said with a very mischievous grin.

Gripping her satchel, Sonia grinned back. "Oh," she said. "Oh, yes there is. Something really.... magical."

Pam chuckled. "You have a lot of confidence in your abilities, do you? I like that."

"My innate skills are honed to a fine edge," Sonia boasted. "But I have a little extra something which... uh... transforms the occasion. Makes things vastly more pleasurable."

Now Pam looked boggled. "Enlighten me, of master of the pleasurable arts!"

Grinning, Sonia opened her satchel and reached inside. She made a show of withdrawing the little wooden box from inside.

"Oh, wow. Look. A box," Pam said, deadpan. "Not the box I was hoping to see, if you know what I mean."

Sonia chuckled and gave a knowing grin. "What is the purpose of boxes?"

"Uh, to hold things inside them?"

"Correct!" Sonia undid the latch and pulled open the lid. She tilted is so Pam could see inside.

Within the box, couched in thick purple colored velvet lining, was a narrow pink dildo. For some reason, Pam felt there was more to it then that.

"I'm all for dildo's. Used them many times in the past."

"Not like this," said Sonia. She took it out, and placed the wooden box on table. She held it up by its wide, flat base. It was almost completely featureless, no real penis details. Just a simple looking dildo that was wide at the bottom portion, then tapered to a narrow nub at its top.

"This," Sonia said, "is a Futa-Totem."

Pam's eyes shot open wide. "No way!" Shocked. "I'd heard of them before. Even know some friends who... uh... played around with them. Never experienced one myself."

"An experience is exactly what you will have," Sonia offered it to her. "Care to try it out?"

Looking a little sheepish, Pam shook her head. "Maybe later. But for now, you first. I want to see this thing in action!"

"Your wish is my command," said Sonia. She held it out to Pam, "Here, hold it a second will you?"

Pam hesitated, then shrugged and took it. If felt no different than any other dildo she'd handled in the past, of which there had been many. Certainly didn't feel magical.

"What do I do with it?" Pam asked.

Sonia unbuttoned her jeans and then unzipped them. "You are going to stick it up my ass. Sound like fun?"

Pam laughed, "Hell, yeah!"

Sonia turned around and pushed her jeans down to her knees. Given a close up of a magnificently shaped butt, Pam smacked it.

"Okay, you have a little chore to do first," Sonia said.

"And that would be?" Pam said, intrigued.

Sonia bent over. Pam couldn't resist and kissed a cheek. Sonia then reached around with both hands, gripped her ass cheeks, and spread them wide. Her puckered anus presented itself to Pam in all its tasty magnificence.

"Lub me up," Sonia said. She looked back over her shoulder at Pam. "With your tongue only."

Pam was overjoyed, "That is not a chore at all, baby!"

Leaning forward, Pam happily pressed her face up in between Sonia's butt cheeks. She loved the way the skin of the other woman's ass felt against the sides of her face.

Pam gave her asshole a tentative lick. She was happy to see Sonia react by having her asshole pucker a little at being touched. Pam licked again. She spit on it, and watched the bubbly spittle seep down its counters to Sonia's taint. She spit again.

Then, as if her very life depended on it, she licked. Up from the top of Sonia's spit dripping taint, and over her beautiful asshole. Several times she licked it. She gave each lick a hard press so as she could feel a little give with Sonia's glistening asshole.

Soon Sonia could feel she was well and truly lubed up. Spittle even dribbled down the side of one leg. "Okay," Sonia gasped. "Let's do this. Slide it in!"

Pam gave Sonia's asshole one quick final lick, then leaned back a bit. She held the Futa-Totem in one hand and moved it towards Sonia's well licked anus.

In anticipation, Sonia's asshole puckered several times. Pam gently pressed the narrow blunted time of the magical dildo against it. Then, slowly, she slid it in. It did so with little or no resistance. The folds of Sonia's asshole gripped it almost possessively as it entered her.

Finally, it was completely inside her, and only the flat bottom base was left outside, to prevent the thing from totally vanishing inside her.

Sonia gasped and spun around. She stood up, and both women looked at the shaved spot directly above the top of her pussy.

Almost immediately, there appeared a small bulge in Sonia's flesh. Like a finger was poking at it from the inside. That bulge protruded out more. Then, it formed into the perfect shape of a prick!

Pam gasped in amazement. "It's working!" she said.

"Watch!" said Sonia. She was breathing heavy, enjoying the sensation of the process.

The prick started to push outward. Behind it was the girth of a cock's shaft. It was pretty wide. The shaft grow out longer, its fat prick bobbed up and down a little with the forward movement.

Finally, the growth stopped. A magnificent dick now hung from Sonia's groin.

"I'm... I'm speechless," whispered Pam, astounded.

"Not... done... yet," Sonia grunted. She grabbed her new cock and held it up. The skin directly under the shaft's base was forming into a wrinkly sack. It puffed outward. Then, as if conjured out of nothing, two testicles practically popped into existence inside the wrinkly sack.

Sonia's new nut sack quivered with any movement she made.

Sonia sighed, a light sheen of sweat gleamed across her forehead. "Growing a cock and balls can't take a lot out of a girl."

Pam was elated, and clapped with joy. "A-fucking-mazing!" She laughed, getting over the shock of the moment. The things you do not expect to find in the back room of a library.

"So," said Sonia, "Wanna fuck?" She shook her new dick at Pam for emphasis.

Pam glanced up at a clock on the wall. She shook her head, "No time right now. But lets play with it a little, huh? Stuff it down your pants for a sec, I wanna see it burst out!"

Realization dawned on Sonia and she grinned at the prospect of play along. "Cool," she said.

Sonia pulled up her pants and stuffed her new cock down the front but her jeans were too tight, so she had to keep the top button undone. Laughing at the absurdity of how the action must have looked an outsider, she managed to cram her new dick down her pants.

Sonia wanted to ask what was next. Before she could say anything Pam dropped to her knees in front of her. Sonia's eyes widened with excitement, and she practically felt the new cock struggling to be released, like it had a mind of its own.

"Whip it out," Pam said.

*There is a God!* Sonia's brain seemed to cheer at her.

"Hurry," Pam said. "I'm only suppose to be on my coffee break." She looked up at Sonia. "And I wanna little taste, too."

Sonia quickly undid her zipper. Her erect dick practically popped out at Pam with a sudden motion that threatened to poke the librarian in the eye.

Pam giggled a little, but immediately grabbed it. The eagerness of her grip on her new member nearly made Sonia cum right there, but she kept herself from making that mistake and kept her cool.

"Mmmm," Pam said. She very gently kissed the tip of her fat prick. "I like the taste of that." She stuck out her tongue and flickered it against its prick. She did this for several moments, alternating between kissing and flickering at it.

Then, suddenly, Pam opened her mouth wide and lunged forward. Nearly entire length of Sonia's dick was swallowed in one motion. Sonia actually felt her prick slide against the roof of Pam's mouth, and lodge in the back of the other woman's hot throat.

Sonia moaned with ecstasy.

"Mmmm," Pam said again. At least that's what it sounded like. She did have a big cock jammed in her mouth, after all.

Clinching her lips around its girth, Pam began to move her head up and down. She sucked at Sonia's swollen member, gently.

Sonia could feel Pam's determined grip at the base of the shaft and part of her palm against its balls, yet she could also feel the hot sensation of the wonderful wet friction of her new dick sliding in and out of Pam's mouth.

Sonia moaned again. She was now having a heck of a time not cumming and having hot jizz exploding out the back of Pam's head.

"Pam to the front desk please! Pam to the front desk!" suddenly said a loud voice.

They both froze.

It was the intercom.

But Pam didn't lose her cool. Slowly, almost deliberately, she slide up its shaft, which now was slick with her spittle. Pam's sucking lips slide over the prick, but remained locked on the very tip of it. As she looked up at Sonia she felt her tongue flicker feather-like at the tip.

Then Pam pulled it out and gave it one last quick kiss. She stood, and Sonia found herself standing in front of her holding her spit covered, erect dick. *Was it over?*

"This is not over," Pam said, as if reading her thoughts. Pam stood on her tip toes and kissed Sonia on the lips.

"I liked that taste, and I'll be back for more," she said. "Think you can wait for me?" She grinned evilly.

"Yeah!" Sonia gasped. *Sweet Lord Almighty, Yes!*

And with that, Pam slipped out the door, and closed it behind her, locking it.

Sonia was left standing there, pants down to her knees, holding her dick.

Not wanting to rub one out and be unable to follow through later, she stuffed her cock back into her pants. There was literally nothing for her to do back here, so to avoid a feeling of foolishness she spent the time reading while waiting.

It didn't take long. Soon, some of the lights went off, but a bank of them stayed on in the back room. Closing time.

Then, after what seemed like forever, the door clicked open, and for a brief moment, Sonia thought someone other than Pam was going to come in and find him there.

It wasn't. Face beaming, Pam entered, and relocked the door behind her.

"Well, well, well," Pam said. "Tired of waiting?"

Sonia sprang to her feet from the chair she had been reading in. "Nope, not at all. Uh, are we alone now?"

She smiled. "Yes, and let me prove it." Suddenly, in one fluid motion, she pulled off her shirt. Sonia was rendered speechless, as she was not wearing a bra (which Sonia had suspected), and her small, perky breasts presented themselves to the world to be admired.

Sonia also couldn't help but notice she had a flat, well defined tummy.

"Wow," Sonia said.

"It gets better," with a couple of quick motions, Pam pulled down her jeans, as well as her thong panties, down to her ankles. She grinned at Sonia as she kicked off her shoes, and stepped out of everything.

Eager to join in the festivities, Sonia quickly pulled off her own shirt, and tossed it. Then she started on her pants, but Pam walked over to her, and put her hands on Sonia's hand, stopping her. Sonia's eyes were on the trim triangle of hair that was between her well muscled thighs.

"Wait, not yet," she said, rubbing the growing bulge in Sophia's pants.

Certain Sonia would do as she asked, Pam sashayed over to the desk. Sonia's eyes were locked on that amazingly firm butt, and the tiny peek of a pussy they presented.

Pam glanced back at her, then bent straight over the desk, so her elbows were leaning on the top. Wiggling her ass, Sonia could now see the well shaved pinkness of her pussy. "I want you to spank me," Pam said. "I've been a very, very bad girl."

Transfixed by the movement of Pam's naked flesh and that wondrous ass, Sonia walked up behind her. Impulsively, she cupped Pam's buttocks. *Sweet Nirvana!* He thought.

Sonia wanted to fuck her so hard, right then and there, but decided to play along. Holding up a hand at the ready, Sonia looked at her for her queue.

"Spank me," Pam said. So Sonia did, with a light slap. First one cheek, and then the other. She really enjoyed how her firm buttocks moved when she did so.

Pam shuddered, and said, "Harder! And don't be a pussy about it!"

*Well, okay then*, Sonia thought.

She did, this time a little harder, and using her full palm, not just the fingers. Pam yelped, and Sonia found her hand actually stung.

"More!"

"Yes, Ma'am!" Sonia said, and did so. Over and over she smacked her lovely ass, until it progressed to a full on spanking. Each time Pam yelped, or groaned. She even gritted her teeth to keep from screaming out, but that didn't last long as Sonia kept at it. Smack, smack, smack.

Pam raised a hand. "Okay, okay," she panted. "Stop!"

Disappointed, Sonia did. "Did I hurt you?" She hadn't wanted to have this kinky little exercise end due to her being overzealous.

"No," Pam said. "Not yet." She grinned evilly.

Sonia nearly had an orgasm from Pam's expression alone.

"Not yet?" Sonia echoed, oblivious to the meaning, but wanting to know more, all the same.

Pam pointed to one of the carts, which was full of thick hardcovers. "Grab a classic."

Obeying, she walked over to it, feeling her wetness around the crotch of her jeans chaff roughly against her skin. She picked out a book from the cart selection; it was a flimsy and small mass market edition.

"How about this?" Sonia asked.

Pam's panting had lessened, and she was using a hand to reach around and massage her the bright red skin of her ass. "Is it a classic?"

"Classic?" Sonia looked. "Uh, it's about medicine or something."

Pam had moved a finger over her raw pussy, and she flinched with ecstasy at the painful touch. "No, not that one. Get something good, something that has meaning."

Confused at the request, but not wanting to question it for fear of putting a sudden end to this wonderful encounter, Sonia picked out another book.

"The Complete Dickens Collection," she said hefting the large tome. It was thick and weighed a good couple pounds.

Pam nodded with a smile, one finger teasing the wetness of her pussy around. "That will do. It has the word dick in it."

Sonia actually laughed out loud. Pam laughed too.

Sonia was not going to argue this, so she stood behind Pam, and to one side. *Fuck she looks hot*, she thought. Her new dick was now practically bursting out of her jeans. Pam had braced her arms on the desk again, in preparation of the wonderful pain.

Sonia gripped the big book with both hands, and hoisted it over one shoulder. This view accentuated the wonder curve of Pam's buttock muscles, and again, Sonia yearned to fuck her hard with her new dick. But that will have to wait just a little while longer.

"I'd really like to fuck the hell out you right now," Sonia admitted. She almost regretted blurting it out, but God damn this chick looked fuckable as all hell.

Pam winked at her over her shoulder, "Soon. Very, very soon. But first, do this to me. I need it to get going." She smiled.

God, I am one lucky girl, Sonia thought. Her face actually hurt from grinning so much.

"Ready?" Sonia asked.

Without saying anything, Pam faced forward again, and nodded her head vigorously. She was psyching herself up.

Pam took a deep breath. Sonia took a deep breath, too.

Sonia swung hard aiming at the curving muscle of her ass, directly from behind.

Pam grunted, but gritted her teeth. And Sonia smacked her again, then again. Over and over. The movement made the Futa-Totem in her ass throb.

At first, Pam kept the noise she made to a minimum, but as Sonia kept spanking her with the big book, she started to get louder. Soon, she was almost shouting with each and every smack.

Pam's body would even quiver with the anticipation of each hit. But she didn't tell Sonia to stop. She only flinched, making her small pert breasts jiggle.

Eventually, she raised her hand again, and Sonia stopped. She was breathing too hard from the shrieking to say anything at first. Sonia lowered the book, and waited. She looked so damned fuckable.

"Okay, okay!" Pam was gasping. "Now get some Shakespeare!"

*Was she kidding? When were they gonna fuck?* Sonia thought, incredulous. But she did as she was asked. When a hot, naked chick, who is bent over begging to be spanked and spanked hard, asks you to do something that turns her on even more; you did it, damn it!

Sonia quickly found a Shakespearean collection, and it was twice the size of the other. Sonia's eyes widened as she hefted it. "Are you sure?" she asked, concerned.

"Yeah," Pam said, nodding quickly. "Do it now before I change my mind! Spank my ass with it!"

Again, Sonia smacked her, again Pam shrieked with pain and delight. Sonia repeated this over and over until she was certain the bright red skin on Pam's ass was going to burst from all that punishment.

This time, she did not last as long as previously before she raised her hand, and Sonia stopped.

Sonia found her fingers actually started to hurt, where they got caught between the book and the firm flesh of Pam's ass. Sonia could even see they made a couple of impressions on Pam's lovely skin. Red on red.

Pam was gasping for air, and her whole body quivered and shook. *Is she having an orgasm?* Sonia thought.

"Okay," Pam said, gulping in air. "Strip! Show me that piece of meat of yours!"

Sonia did not require any further coaxing, and her shoes, pants and panties flew in different directions within seconds.

Her new dick was standing at full attention. "What do you think?" Sonia asked.

"I think you should bring that thing over here," Pam said.

Bent over as she was, her pussy was pushed out, glistening. Sonia could see she was very wet, to the point where it dribbled all down her pussy lips, and partially down one of her inner thighs.

Sonia's mouth watered just looking at it.

"Eat me, first," Pam said. "Lick me all up."

All right! Sonia got down on her knees, lightly gripped Pam's red ass, spreading the rounded cheeks a little. Then she licked her; nice and long at first, from the bottom to the top. *Or was it top to the bottom from this angle?* Sonia thought.

She tasted incredible and Sonia told her so. Her pussy was sopping wet from being turned on so much from the spanking. Sonia could feel the heat of the blood brought so close to the surface of her red skin, rubbing against her face and chin. She licked her for several long tasty minutes until Pam was moaning again. Sonia could feel her wetness all over her chin, and some dribbled a little down her throat.

Careful, she sucked out her clit between her lips, and it was Sonia's turn to use her tongue for flickering.

Pam arched her back, groaning. Occasionally she pushed back so Sonia's face was forced deeper inside her incredible wetness, and Sonia nearly went mad with the feeling of it.

Sonia worked on Pam's pussy like this for a long time, sucking up her lips so their soft folds slipped in gently between her teeth. Pam's entire body shuddered and quaked. Eventually, she couldn't handle any more, and said, "Fuck me!"

Pam looked over her shoulder at Sonia's eyes that peeked over the curvature of her ass. "Fuck me with your cock!"

Sonia stood up, grabbed her dick (or was it Dickens?) and put her other hand on Pam's ass. Then, very slowly, she slide its large swollen prick into her. Sonia bit her bottom lip because she nearly hit the came by accident right there.

Taking a moment to gather herself, Sonia then slid the entire length into her. Pam gasped. She felt so damn good; very hot, and very wet. Then Sonia slid back her cock the full length until it was nearly out, and slammed it back in all the way. Pam grunted. Sonia did it again. And again.

Sonia pumped her, hard as Pam had asked her to. She marvelled at the the bright redness of her ass, and gazed down appreciatively at her little puckered asshole. Sonia rubbed at with a thumb, all the while not stopping with her rhythm. Pam's flesh jiggled, but was so firm it barely moved.

Pam tossed her head back and forth, occasionally arching her back all the way so Sonia could reach around and squeeze her firm little tits. At one point Sonia pulled Pam back by the elbows so she was almost standing up straight, and slammed her pussy harder and harder.

Soon, after all that had happened, and with the incredible sensation of being finally inside her, Sonia knew couldn't hold it any longer.

"Ah, fuck!" Sonia groaned loudly.

Pam instinctively knew what this meant, reached back and gently pushed at Sonia's stomach so she eased her cock out of her. Pam's pussy made wet noises as if in protest.

Spinning around, she dropped to her knees in front of Sonia, and as Sonia stroked its shaft, Pam slurped the dick into her hot mouth. She sucked furiously until Sonia practically screamed as she finally came into Pam's hungry mouth.

Somehow Pam managed to chuckle while sucking the her off. Sonia's hips bucked with her orgasm, fucking Pam's mouth. When Sonia was nearly spent, Pam swallowed loudly, never letting the cock out of her mouth. Sonia sagged against the desk as Pam continued to nurse the load.

"Whoa," Sonia said. She could feel her body was covered in sweat from such wonderful exertion.

Pam pulled Sonia's dick out of her mouth with a wet pop, and said, "Well, Sonia. Thanks for the fun. This really topped off my day." She smiled and returned to sucking the other woman dry.

Chuckling, Sonia couldn't agree more!

END

# Futa Rama (Futa-Totem)

Shelly faced a long, and boring drive through the countryside as she headed south to visit family for the holidays.

She found the radio annoying as it continuously played sappy love songs over and over, so she just turned off. Unfortunately, this left her with her thoughts and memories of her recently failed relationship with her ex-life partner, Janice. They had been married for less than three years but she knew it had been doomed from the start. The passion that initially attracted them to each other faded quickly and they simply fell into the routine of having each other around. Even the use of the Futa-Totem, and the incredible pleasures it created for them, was not enough.

And it was passion Shelly wanted more of in her life, and since there was no more with Janice she made the painful decision of cancelling the whole thing. They separated only last month and filed the divorce paperwork. And despite being amicable it was still quite stressful. They had fought over who got to keep the Totem, and they agreed to share ownership of it, alternating every other month.

Now the little wooden box that held it, was stuffed snuggly in Shelly's purse, on the seat next to her. Never want that to be too far out of reach, in case an opportunity should arise.

The early morning sun gave an orange hew to the sky, and tinged the countless trees that strobe by her on both sides of the winding country road. There was very little traffic, which was why she purposely took this more scenic route to her parents house several states away. She did not mind peacefulness but having Janice around for so many years she found a lack of another person's presence daunting.

She had no one else in her life at the moment to fill the void. Neither she nor Janice were unfaithful to the other during their failing relationship. And having only just recently separated she had neither the time, nor the will to find someone.

What she really craved was someone to find her. A distraction of the momentary kind. If she had to be completely honest, she really wanted to put the Futa-Totem to good use. Just have fun. She did not think she had the emotional toolkit to deal with anything too heavy beyond that.

"I just need a new woman," she said to herself. Shelly laughed at the absurdity of that declaration. She wasn't gonna find anyone at her parent's house, that was for certain. And she sure as hell didn't think anyone was waiting for her out here, in the middle of nowhere.

She peered up at the mountains, each covered with an apron of thick forest, that she slowly past by. "Nope," she said. "Only thing out here are wild mountain women and Bigfoot. And both would be too smelly for my taste."

As Shelly mind wandered, she concentrated less on the road. At a particularly sharp turn, a figure suddenly appeared directly in front of her. A *woman*, walking dangerously close to the edge of the road.

Shelly yelped, and yanked at the wheel, swerving to avoid the other woman. Her car fish tailed and she fought to control it. Pumping the brakes she managed to avoid flying off the road and into the trees. Always a cautious driver, she had not been travelling too fast and she skidded to a stop directly on the meridian facing the direction she had been coming from.

Her fingers were dug into the steering wheel and her hair was now in her face, which puffed out as she breathed heavily.

*Is that what it's like to almost die?*, she thought. She barked out a laugh, still in shock.

It was only after a few moments of recovering that she realized someone was running towards the car. The stupid chick!

*Oh, I'm going to tear a strip out of her!*, Shelly thought as she released her vice like grip from the steering wheel, and pushed back her hair.

Her eyes widened in surprise as the other woman got closer. *Sweet Lord,* Shelly thought. *This chick looks like one of those bikini models you see on bus shelter poster ads for vacations. What the heck was she doing way out here?*

Shelly found the wherewithal to roll down the window as the chick ran up to her driver's side door. Her stunningly beautiful face was only slightly marred by her expression of concern.

"What's an bikini model doing way out here?" Shelly blurted. She put her hand to her mouth and she gasped at her own stupidity. "Was that my outside voice?"

The chick didn't seem to hear her, and said, "Are you all right? Are you hurt at all?" Her voice was soft and lyrical. Her light jacket emphasized her slim frame, and her jeans did little to hide lean muscular thighs. For some bizarre reason her body reminded Shelly of the thin trees all around them, lean and strong.

*Like a wild mountain woman's!*

"Yes," Shelly finally managed to say. "I think I'm alive." Shelly grinned up at her.

The chick sagged with relief, smiling for the first time, and Shelly found her perfect teeth out did the brightness of the morning sun.

"Well, that's relief," the chick said, placing her hands on the rolled down window. She could not help but notice how delicate they looked.

Shelly caught herself wondering just how gentle those little hands could be, moving up and down her body.

"I am so sorry," the chick said. "It was my fault. I didn't realize I was so close to the road, I was avoiding the mud and my mind wandered."

"Oh, no, it was my fault," Shelly said. "I wasn't paying attention, my thoughts drifted..." and as she said that she realized her drifting thoughts had been about a much needed woman to distract her from her troubles. Shelly looked up at her beautiful face, with its perfect features and bright smile. *And I go ahead and nearly kill the only woman for miles!*

The chick was looking at her, smiling when Shelly had a thunderous revelation.

"Hey," Shelly said sweetly. "Since I almost splattered you all over the road, the least I could do is offer you a ride." She felt her face reddening as she spoke, trying not make it obvious what kind of ride she really had in mind.

The chick arched a brow, considering the offer. Finally, she said, "Where are you headed?"

"South. A long way south, actually."

The chick frowned a little and Shelly was momentarily mortified she would lose her. But again, the chick regarded her with that sexy arch of the eyebrow. "I'm actually heading east, and the turnoff road I'll be taking is only a couple of miles further up the road." She shrugged as if to suggest she really didn't want to bother Shelly any more.

Oh, she could bother her, alright.

Shelly grinned. "I'll take you to the turn off. It might keep me from running you over again when I turn around."

The chick laughed. "Okay. You win. Just let me grab my backpack." She trotted away where her pack lay at the side of the road. She had obviously dropped it when Shelly nearly hit her.

Shelly watched the movement of her butt in her jeans as she moved.

*Yum, yum, yum*, Shelly thought. *Love to tap that with a magical cock!*

Shelly turned the car around in a wide arch, to point back in the southerly direction she was original travelling. This time she didn't almost kill the bikini model.

Shelly watched as the chick grabbed her backpack. Shelly's heart was pounding excitedly in her chest. She looked at herself in the rear view mirror, and made a vain attempt at fixing her tussled hair. She locked eyes with herself.

*Do you know what you are doing girl?* She grinned. *Yes, I'm going to be doing her! Balls deep all the way!*

The chick came back, and threw her pack in the backseat. Shelly took her purse and put it on the floor next to her seat. The Futa-Totem's wooden box peeked out at her.

Then the chick sat down in the passenger side, closing the door. As she settled in, Shelly sneaked a peak at her now that she was up close.

*Yup*, she thought, *she definitely a babe.* With that confirmed, she now had to find out if she could see more of that body.

The chick turned and smiled at Shelly, offering her hand.

"I'm Zoey."

Shelly took it, and tried not to shiver with the electric touch of her.

"Shelly."

They shook.

Shelly found she was unwilling to release her hand right away. But when she arched that brow again and added that cute smile, Shelly relented. She pulled out on the road and drove, trying mightily to keep her eyes from staring at Zoey.

They made very idle chit chat, of which none involved her getting naked, and Zoey spanking her. Shelly was just trying to work up the courage to make it happen. Yet, she got the distinct sense Zoey was intrigued by her. Maybe even found her attractive.

It only took a few minutes but they arrived at Zoey's turnoff, and begrudgingly she pulled over. She placed the car in park.

They smiled nervously at one another.

"Well," Zoey said. "This is me. Thanks for the lift."

She opened the door to get out.

*Stop her!* Shelly thought.

"Hey, what's that over there," she said pointing towards what looked like the entrance to an old dirt road that disappeared into the forest.

Zoey paused and looked. "Looks like a switchback road," she said. "Runaway truck use them in an emergency."

"Wow. I've never seen one of those maybe I'll go down a little ways just to check out. Would be nice and private." Shelly looked at her meaningfully. "Care to come have an emergency with me?" *An emergency of the Futa kind?*

Zoey paused with the door open slightly and one foot on the road. Her eyebrows had raised in surprise making her look all the more adorable.

A second passed and then another, each feeling like years to Shelly.

Zoey chuckled slightly, then settled back in her seat and close the door. She then regarded Shelly with a seductive smile. "That's a fantastic idea," she said.

Shelly laughed.

Hoping not to lose her in the moment, Shelly quickly took the car out of park and steered it onto the switchback road.

She drove slowly down the gravel road while fully conscious of the glances Zoey was giving her. The moment the highway seemed a safe distance out of view, she pulled over as far as she could and parked, again.

She turned the car off, and killed the power, too, and sat back.

They both grinned nervously at each other.

"Well," Shelly said. "What do we do now?"

Zoey made a show of looking around at their surroundings. "I dunno. Is this the spot you normally take the women you almost run over?"

Shelly laughed, undid her seat belt. She reached into her purse on the floor. "I have a little something here I save for special occasions just like this."

Zoey grinned. "This is special is it?"

"Almost running over a sexy babe in the middle of the forest, and then taking her roadside to fuck her brains out does constitute a special occasion, yes," Shelly said, smiling.

She pulled out the little wooden box and held is so Zoey could get a good look.

Zoey looked perplexed. "What is it?"

"A box."

"Ha ha, funny lady. Whatcha got inside it?"

Shelly undid the boxes latch and opened the lid. Inside, cushioned in velvet, was what looked like a narrow pink dildo with a wide flat base.

Zoey laughed. "A dildo, huh? You always carry one around with you on your travels?"

Shelly arched a brow. "Not just any dildo. This one is very special. It has... uh... unique properties." She took it out and put the box on the dash. She held it up by its flat base. It was all pink, wide near the bottom, and narrowed to a blunt tip at the top.

"Okay, care to enlightened the unenlightened? What sort of magical properties?"

Shelly frowned a little. Then asked, "Have you ever heard of a Futa-Totem?"

Zoey gasped. "A *Futa-Totem*? Are you kidding me?" She looked at the pink dildo with more respect.

"So you have heard of it?"

Zoey nodded, looking considerably more eager than when the conversation started. "You bet! Just never thought I'd see one in real life before." She was ready for a little roadside fun with this beautiful woman, but this Futa-Totem just catapulted things to a whole new level. A whole new stratosphere!

Shelly nodded, sagely. "A Futa virgin are you? Perfect."

Zoey smiled, "How so?"

Shelly grinned mischievously. "You get to try it out first."

Eyes widened, Zoey said, "Really?"

"Yes, really."

"So, it really works? No bullshit? I'll grow a magic dick and everything?"

"And everything."

Zoey was all game now. "Okay, what do I do?"

"First, pull her pants down. Need to get to your asshole."

"Okay!" Zoey said, elated.

Shelly chuckled, holding the Futa-Totem at the ready.

Zoey deftly undid her pants, and wiggled in her seat as she pulled them down past her knees. She had wonderfully muscled thighs, just the way Shelly likes them.

Then Zoey pushed her pelvis up from the seat, and slid her panties down, too. She sat back down and looked at Shelly with anticipation.

Shelly said, "Feet up on the dash."

Zoey did so. She exposed a small thatch of well trimmed brown pubic hair. Shelly liked them well groomed. Also, her clean pink pussy awaited. She was already getting wet.

But Shelly wanted something a little more. "Bend you knees back more."

Doing so, gave Shelly a good look at Zoey's asshole, nestled between the firm, smooth curves of her ass cheeks.

"Beautiful," Shelly said. Unable to help herself, she pushed down on Zoey's leg, so as to get easier access, an leaned forward. She gave Zoey's musty little clam a nice long lick from side to side.

Zoey moaned. Shelly licked some more. Because her her angle, she lapped at it sideways. Zoey's lovely pussy lips spread with little effort from Shelly's probing tongue.

Shelly lapped hungrily for a few minutes. Then she realized she was still holding the Futa-Totem. "Oops," she said. "Got lost in the moment."

Zoey was smiling easily, having enjoyed her cunt being licked. "No, problem."

Shelly turned her attention to Zoey's little asshole, which seemed to be waiting patiently. Shelly spit on it. Spittle pooled around it, filling its little puckered contours. She spit again, this time heavier.

Satisfied, she then angled the Futa-Totem, and aimed it at the cute little butt hole. "You ready?" she asked.

"Yeah," Zoey whispered. "Do it." She shuddered in anticipation.

Shelly then gently poked the narrow nub of the Totem's tip into Zoey's asshole. She slowly slid it down and inside. Zoey's anus accepted the magical dildo with ease. Finally, only the flat bottom of its base was all that was outside of Zoey.

"Oh, my!" said Zoey.

Shelly sat up. Zoey pushed herself up, too. Her legs splayed out by the car pedals.

They both looked at the spot directly about Zoey's pussy, where her pubic hair was.

"Do you feel it?" Shelly asked. She knew what it felt like having done this so many wonderful times.

Zoey nodded, eyes wide, eye brows up in amazement. "It... it tickles."

"It's going to do more than that in just one second."

She was right. At that exact moment, a small round bump appeared in Zoey's skin under her pubic hair. It grew larger, and rounder in the next moment.

"Whoa," said Zoey.

"That ain't nothing yet."

The bump pushed out more, then instantly formed itself into something else. Now a fat, purple prick poked out from Zoey's belly, surrounded by her pubic hair. Like a mushroom in some grass.

Then, it started to push upwards. Behind this magically formed fat prick, was the beginnings of a cock's shaft. Inch by inch it grew out of Zoey.

Both women watched this transformation occur, completely transfixed by what they were seeing. Zoey more so than Shelly. But Shelly found it just as incredible this time as she did the very first time she experienced this. Cocks magically growing out of people have that effect.

Then, at about a good 10 inches, the dick stopped growing outward.

"Wow!" Zoey exclaimed.

Shelly held up a hand. "Wait for it."

Just then, a wrinkly scrotum sack ballooned out from below the base of the new cock's shaft. Zoey laughed. "I get balls, too?"

Then, one testicle literally popped into existence on one side of the ball sack. Them the other did to. They dangled there, like to happy peas in a pod.

"Holy. Shit." Zoey said. She gripped her new cock, testing its size and heft. "I'm hung like a horse!"

"It really cums, too," said Shelly with a very wide grin.

"No way!" Zoey squealed.

"Functions just like any other man's junk. Only this is yours to do with as you please."

Zoey shook her massive new cock and said, "I got a function for it." She looked at Shelly. "I think you have to make things up to me, since you nearly killed me before. If you don't mind." She grinned.

"I don't mind one bit," Shelly said, and moved closer to her. Placing a hand on Zoey's shoulder she whispered in her ear, "Yes, I would like to suck your new big fat dick, as an apology." To ensure she did not miss her meaning, she grabbed Zoey's cock; it was firm and erect. She kissed the tip several times, feeling its firmness in her hand. Gently, she started to lick its length, up and down from the base of its shaft to the swollen prick. Like a lollipop.

Zoey gasped softly, putting one hand on the back of Shelly's head to guide her up and down movements.

Zoey then reached down, found the release for the chair and angled it back some more, giving Shelly more room to work on her properly.

With its knob glistening from her diligent licking, Shelly then took Zoey's fat prick into her mouth, pushing it up to the back of her throat as far as it would go. Her lips firmly gripped its shaft as they moved closer to the base, her nose touched Zoey's stomach. Then she sucked at it, moving her head up and down all the way. She stroked the dick with her hand, following it with her lips.

"Now that's a talent," Zoey whispered, then moaned.

For several long wonderful minutes Shelly sucked Zoey's new cock, until she reached a point she was certain she was going to shoot her load. The car filled with sound of her hard sucking, and hungry slurping.

Carefully, Shelly slowed, not wanting her to be spent too soon. Kissing the tip of the prick one more time, she then looked up at Zoey with a big smile.

She said, "Let's fuck."

Zoey smiled back, but offered that cute arching brow again. "It's a little crowded in here for that, don't you think?"

She sat up a little and said, "Well, we do need some elbow room. Let's take this party outside."

And with that they jumped out of the car. Before Zoey moved around towards her, Shelly pointed at her and commanded, "Strip lady!"

Zoey laughed, but did as she was told, stripping her clothes off, her erect cock quivering with each motion.

Shelly did the same, deftly peeling off all her clothing in under a minute. They threw their clothes into the car. The gravel felt cool under their feet.

Zoey walked quickly around to Shelly's side of the car, holding her stiff dick.

"I want you to fuck me this way," Shelly said, motioning for her to get behind her.

Shelly stood standing with her arms braced, one against the open door, the other against the car roof. She spread her legs out a little and stuck her butt out, arching her back.

Zoey smacked her ass, and moved up behind her. Holding her new cock, she rubbed its prick along the inside folds of her pussy, exploring her wetness, teasing her with it.

When Shelly could no longer stand the anticipation commanded, "Fuck me! Just fuck me, dammit!"

"Okay," Zoey said, and suddenly lunged forward, jamming the entire length of her massive dick inside her with one motion. She felt the Futa-Totem in her ass throb and tingle.

Shelly gasped, and gritted her teeth as Zoey immediately started to pound against her. Her braced arms tensed with each impact. She delighted in knowing that if she hadn't held herself in such a way, Zoey may very well of fucked her straight through the door with those powerful thrusts.

Zoey pounded against her, over and over, until Shelly's moans grew louder and more intense. Her flesh grew red where Zoey smashed up against her. Zoey smacked her ass repeatedly, slapping both in turn.

As she continued to fuck Shelly, Zoey licked her thumb and then rubbed it against Shelly's little ass-hole. She circled it with her thumb over and over.

Several minutes passed as Zoey worked on her, and the forest filled with the sounds of their passionate efforts. Shelly moaned, and occasionally yelped when she smacked her reddening flesh. Zoey gasped, she was desperately trying to not cum just yet.

When Zoey was close to being spent she slowed, easing in and out of Shelly gently. Zoey reached up and cupped Shelly's tits, which were perky and firm. She squeezed them, and pinched at their erect nipples.

Then, Zoey pulled out of her, and smacked her ass loudly one more time.

"Ow!" Shelly cried with delight.

"I want to eat your pussy," Zoey said pointing towards the hood of the car.

She glowed. "Great idea!"

Shelly giggled as she tiptoed to the front of the car. Zoey followed in hot pursuit. The hood was sloped and Shelly eased herself up it by wiggling her bum. Then she leaned back on her elbows and spread her legs.

The fibreglass popped and sagged with her weight.

"I don't think this car was designed for this," Shelly said, not caring in the least.

"Let's see what else it wasn't designed for," Zoey said with mischievous smile. Zoey squatted in front of her, and the Futa-Totem seemed to pulse in her ass. She placed her hands against Shelly's widened thighs, then Zoey leaned forward and gave her shaved pussy a nice long welcoming lick.

Then she licked again, and again, until she developed a rhythm. Shelly bent her head back and smiled gloriously up at the blue morning sky, enjoying the sensation of her tongue all over her pussy.

Eventually, Zoey sucked on one of her fingers to get it wet, then she cautiously slipped it up inside Shelly, and she gasped. Then she started to make a come-hither motion against the sensitive pad just behind her pubic bone. Shelly shivered with pleasure, practically seeing stars before her eyes with the intensity.

Zoey returned to work, concentrating more now on her clit. She sucked at it, tickling it with her tongue at the same time. All the while, Shelly gasped with pleasure, squeezing her tits, pinching at their erect nipples. She took one in her mouth and teethed it, sucking.

Zoey ate her out for long moments, listening to the wet sounds her gyrating finger made inside her.

When she had her fill she then stood, big dick still hard and ready. Zoey leaned forward, so she was hovering over Shelly, and pushed her dick downward as far as it would go. She stuck its prick into Shelly's waiting pussy. Shelly gasped, and grabbed onto Zoey's hips.

"You want this?" Zoey asked.

"Yes!" she begged. "Fuck the hell outta me!"

And with that, Zoey suddenly slammed the entire length of her long cock deep inside her. Shelly gasped with the hard penetration. Zoey then lifted her ass up again, so her entire dick was nearly unsheathed from her, and slammed it down again.

The hood of the car popped and squawked with the hard pressured movements.

Over and over Zoey did this, getting faster and faster. Shelly moaned with each pelvic thrust. Long wonderful minutes passed as Zoey slammed her pussy again and again. Eventually, the intensity got to be so much Shelly's eyes rolled upwards, completely lost in the rapture of the moment.

Over and over; again and again Zoey slammed down onto her.

Zoey could not keep up the relentless pace. She enjoyed the feeling of the rubbing wet friction inside Shelly, and seeing her face grimace with the concentrated effort of their passion, Zoey found herself about to orgasm.

"I'm gonna cum!" Zoey finally shouted.

Quickly, Shelly pushed her back, unsheathing Zoey from her.

Zoey stood before her, stroking her cock vigorously. Sitting on the edge of the hood, Shelly leaned forward so she could place the bottom of her open mouth against the base of Zoey's fat prick. Her tongue tickled at it eagerly, and her eyes stared up at Zoey with hunger.

Zoey stroked faster, and soon came with a loud moan. Hot cum spat out all over Shelly; squirting into her mouth which slid down her tongue and pooled at the back of her throat. Over her face in long sticky strands that splayed across her cheeks and forehead. In the corner of one eye, down her chin, and Zoey even got some in her hair.

As Zoey sagged with completion, Shelly made a dramatic show of swallowing.

Shelly smacked her mouth, and rolled her tongue around her lips, getting every white bit. It tasted even better than the real thing. A long thick strand still hung from her chin as she grinned widely at Zoey.

Shelly then grabbed the cock again, and sucked it, nursing the last of its load.

Looking up at Zoey's beautiful face, seeing the sunshine glint off the sweat on her pert tits, Shelly came to a conclusion:

She needed pick up hitchhikers more often!

END

# Have Futa, Will Travel (Futa-Totem)

The very first thing I did, right after landing in Thailand, was get laid.

Call it habit, or maybe tradition, but I've done this with every visit to this wonderful beautiful destination. It might have to do with all the pent up anticipation, or frustration, of getting to play with some of the world's most beautiful Asian girls. God knows, it is something that is constantly on my mind, from the moment I leave the country until my return.

Besides, can you think of a better way for a girl like me to be welcomed into a new country? I mean, really?

But what really helps is the little Futa surprise I will have for the lucky girl, or girls, I will hook up with. That's always been a blast.

Upon my arrival I ran the gambit of customs. "Business or pleasure?" the officer with the off kilter hat asked. "Pleasure," I said smiling. He offered a little frown. Whether it was because he suspected I was a lesbian (and a smoking hot one at that!), or it was just his usual expression. Immigration is a thankless occupation after all. Could not fault the guy.

He stamped my passport and waved me through, and picked up my luggage.

And sure enough, I was stopped at customs. Was it something I was wearing? Anyways, the little sweaty customs dude rummaged through all my stuff, pawing my undies and lingering over my lingerie.

Then, he noticed the little engraved wooden box I had stuffed in my makeup bag.

"What this?" he asked, frowning at it suspiciously.

*What this, indeed,* I thought. "Nothing. Just a wood carving."

Not placated, he undid the little silver clasp, and swung open the lid. Looking inside, he became more confused. He reached in and pulled *it* out.

"This carving?" he asked. He was holding the pink futa-totem up with two fingers by its flat base. To everyone passing by, and looking at this thing the fat idiot was waving around, they would know it as a little dildo. Its shape was smooth, and almost featureless, rounded part way from the bottom, drawing to a dull nub at its tip.

*Its a fucking magic dildo, you shit-head!* I wanted to scream, but held my tongue.

Then, the little toadie sniffed it.

I tried to think on the diplomatic implications if I suddenly jammed the futa-totem right up his chubby butt. But, again, I didn't react. Just nodded.

Giving the futa-totem one final grimace, he returned it to the box, dropping it in my open luggage. He then waved me through.

Determined not to let that little encounter discourage me from enjoying myself, I quickly said thank you, and marched away.

I bypassed the arrivals exit, and cut through the airport and out the departures door. Having been here several times, I knew from experience that the cabbies at the arrivals side charged more for their services. Departures cabbies, ones dropping off customers, are more prone to give a decent price, since they were going to return to the city anyways.

I found a cabbie willing to haggle a little, and we were off.

Thailand was awash with activity. I watched as the organized chaos that was Bangkok streamed by. It was a whirl of honking cars, crazy driving and masses of people all fighting to use the same road. And sweet lord was it hot out. Thankfully, I had arrived prepared, already wearing shorts, a loose shirt and sandals. I was hot, both figuratively and literally.

Eventually, we arrived at my prearranged hotel, located only a few blocks from the some night life bars, which could really be found all around the city.

As I got out of the cab and retrieved my luggage, the driver thrust a weathered photo into my hand. "You like? Nice girls. Very cheap."

It showed a lineup of scantily clad Thai girls staring at the camera. They looked bored, but hot damn were they cute.

I wondered how many others tourists before me, with their sweaty horny hands, had held this photo. Judging by its condition, I would guess many. Dozens, maybe even hundreds.

I politely said no, and paid him. I'd get my own in my own way. Then I checked in.

The bed was queen-size and low to the ground. No doubt for kneeling action. You know you're in the right hotel when the beds are specifically constructed for the maximum sexual positions.

Perfect.

After dumping my gear, and putting my valuables, as well as the futa-totem in the little in-room safe, I went outside and immediately started to prowl.

Walking around, and noticed a lot of pudgy, ugly white men waddling around. I hoped that as a sexy white woman from a far away land, I was a unique encounter for a beautiful Thai girl to choose. I know I would pick me for a random tryst!

I've had some amazing sex with other stunning women. And mostly thanks to this country: Thailand. God Bless this country and its openness to alternative sexual lifestyles. I've always had a thing for Asian women, too, so that is a bonus. The mystic behind their alluring gaze, or the supple sheen of their skin.

It was time to get me one.

Three blocks over I came across a small bar, one of the hundreds here in this city. Thais love to drink! Because it was still the middle of the day, most of the patrons were sitting outside, smoking, and chatting. There were maybe half a dozen women sitting in a small group to one side, and I took a few moments as I approached to find one to my liking. Fortune favours the bold, after all.

They were all cute. Each and every one. But one in particular caught my eye, and, as a bonus, she was the first one to smile as I walked up to them.

"Hi," I said cheerfully. They all giggled or tittered to each other. Here was a strange (yet sexy!) foreign woman with the brass balls to just walk up and talk. I hope I would be rewarded for such behaviour.

Now, walking up to a table full of drop dead gorgeous, overly sexy young women, is not my strong suit. In fact, I'd never have done it back home, that's for damn sure. Or maybe I did but was too drunk and filled with liquid courage. I am incredibly shy, but this place really fuels my confidence. This was only justified by their reaction to me. All of the girls gave a bright hello back, their smiles like a string of Christmas lights.

God, I love Thailand.

I sauntered up that first girl I had noticed, the one who smiled at me as I approached, and she immediately started flirting.

Her name was 'Nah', and I introduced myself as 'Brandi', because real names mattered here as much as your body type did. They don't – in case you still haven't clued in yet.

We chatted, our conversation limited by her small amount of English, and my non-existent Thai. But we both knew the flirtation game and how it was played so the rules were easy to follow.

Once it was established I had found someone I liked the other girls went back to there boredom and chatter. There was no animosity at all. No doubt someone else will come along soon and work up the courage to talk with them, too.

Soon, I had asked if she would come back to my hotel with me, and she hopped out of her stool with a loud "Yes, please!" Well, things couldn't get any better! But, of course, they did.

As we walked I took a moment to give her tight little body a good once over. She was incredibly sexy, and I told her so. She responded by grabbing my elbow and pulling up against me crushing her left breast into my arm. "You sexy, too, Brandi," she said with a giggle.

Good enough for me!

She pulled away and we continued our flirtatious banter. Despite her being a sure thing, it was still fun to have her giggle at my every joke and gives signs of wanting me. This was most definitely a welcome change from the challenges of dating back home.

The front desk clerk didn't so much as give us a glance. Bringing girls into the hotel was par for the course in Thailand after all. One of the other hotels I stayed at previously actually I.D. the girl I was with, just to ensure she was of age, then just waved us through. Women hooking up with other women happened here quite often, apparently. I wondered how many magically grew the occasional dick?

We headed upstairs and I got a good close up look at her butt as she walked up ahead of me. Amazing. So firm and well shaped. I caught myself drooling. She looked back at me occasionally and gave me a sly smile, slowing down so I had no choice but to run into her - her ass pressed up against my stomach. I grabbed her hips then selfishly slid my hands up to cup her breasts. Her lacy bra thwarted me efforts to get a good lay of the land there, but I would soon have those goods, and then some.

At my door she started to tickle me incessantly to the point a couldn't even get the key in the lock.

A male foreigner, and his Thai 'girlfriend' walked by and laughed at our antics. No doubt amused at two women all over each other. Good to see that the love is shared in this place. I wasn't the only one with a stunning bombshell to do with as I pleased. Made me feel part of the group which was the complete opposite of home.

Once inside, I threw on some music and poured us each a drink from a cooler into some plastic cups. She danced around to the music, batting her eyes at me and spinning around in the way that only a girl who lives in night clubs can manage. Sweet lord I was a lucky woman.

As I watched every nuance of her movements I felt a wetness growing between my thighs. Time to get down to business. I had waited long enough (longer that I care to admit).

She grinned at my look and worked her way over to her purse, pulled out a small squeeze bottle of lubricant and a chain of condom packages, and made a show of tossing them on the bed. My kinda girl. Always be prepared.

I was nice and polite, but there was a hungry edge to my voice when I told her to strip naked for me. She giggled but didn't argue, in fact she seemed eager to please me as she began to remove what little clothing she had on. Soon she was practically naked, and man, what a sight she was!

Wearing just a g-string, she gyrated her hips and watched herself with delight in one of the mirrors. I watched her, too. Wow! What an amazing body. Wonderfully pale, small firm breasts with pale coloured nipples. She bent over slightly as she moved and put her hands on her knees, then she rocked her bare pale ass back and forth to the beat of the music.

I couldn't wait any longer. It was time to get the goods. I tossed my empty glass, and she laughed as it clattered on the floor. "I have something for you, all the way from my home country," I purred.

She looked elated. "Really?" she said. "I want!"

"Good!" I said and opened the little safe. She tried to peek over my shoulder but I wouldn't let her, causing her to giggle. Finding what I was looking for, I turned around but kept it hidden behind my back.

She was more than a little curious. "What is it?"

"Something for me, but also for you. I hope you like it." *And are into this kind of thing*, I thought to myself. There was always the possibility she wouldn't like what I was about to show, but it was worth the risk. I could always go to plan B which was fun without my little extra toy. No harm, no foul.

I showed what I was hiding behind my back: the pink futa-totem. I made a 'ta-da' motion with me free hand, as if presenting the grand prize in a game show.

The effect was as intended: Nah was stunned. Her eyes were wide and her mouth hung open. "That is... dido?" she asked, still reeling.

I laughed. "Dildo," I said. "Well, more than that. It's... uh... magical."

She screwed her cute little face up in confusion and I tried not to laugh.

"Here," I said, eager to start the show, "I'll show you what it does."

I undid my belt and unceremoniously dropped my shorts and panties to the knees, then I spun around, practically sticking my ass in her face. With one hand I reached around and grabbed an ass cheek, and pulled it to the side as far as I could giving her a good, thorough, look at my asshole (I bleach, ya know?).

Not quite sure what was expected she smacked my ass. Points to her for at least trying.

"Spit," I said, indicating my anus with a finger. "Lots of spit. Lubricate."

She understood, leaned forward until I could feel her breath on my asshole. Then she spit. A dead on shot for her first go.

"Again," I said. She did. "Again," I repeated. She did, again.

Several times she did this, until I could feel spittle dribbling down my taint, to drip off my pussy. Some sensations you just never get tired of.

"Ok," I said. "Use tongue. Spread it around."

Happily, the little beauty practically crammed her face between my ass cheeks, and used her tongue against my asshole. She gently smeared her spit all over it.

I let this go on for a while. *God damn!*

"Ok, stop," I said. She pulled her head back, and a line of spit extended out from her bottom lip to my taint. Should of taken a picture.

Then, with almost no ceremony, I reached around with my other hand, which was holding the futa-totem. I gently eased the tip in, took a breath, and slid its length all the way inside me, right up to its stopper base.

The effect was almost immediate. Quickly, I turned around to face her, showing her my pussy.

Not knowing what this was about she gave my a perplexed look.

"Wait for it," I breathed, but it was already happening.

Just above my clitoral hood, I bump appeared. Slowly, it started to extend outward from my lower belly. The bump became a fat prick. Then, the shaft of a penis pushed out from behind it. The new appendage elongated to an impressive length, then stopped.

I now had a cock!

But the transformation was not quite complete. A nut sack ballooned out from under the base of my new shaft. Then, one testicle popped into it, then the other, filling out the sack.

Cock and balls! I was ready to rock!

Nah was grinning from ear to ear. She clapped with joy. Since she didn't immediately flee the room screaming, I took that as an okay to continue. Keep the plot moving, as it were.

"It ejaculates, too. Fully functioning for all the fun." I said proudly.

"Dildo," she said, still trying to fathom what she was looking at.

"This is not a dildo. This jammed in my ass is, and it lets this," I pointed at my fantastic new package, "happen."

She nodded. Good to go.

I wanted to role play, so I pulled my panties and shorts back up. My new cock created a huge bulge under the fabric, almost to the point of ripping out of my shorts.

Nah laughed, and I walked back and forth, gyrating my hips. She laughed hysterically. Keep em laughing I always say. Besides, it helped ease her into the fact I was going to ram it deep inside her.

I smiled at her, and asked, "Are you ready for this?" Nah nodded with wide eyed enthusiasm. Perfect!

She waved me over and I moved in with an evil smile on my face. She welcomed me with open arms, hugging me tightly and we danced a little at the foot of the bed. She knew from the look in my eye that it was time for action and she, too, threw her plastic cup away and sat on the bed while I stood in front of her.

She began to undo my shorts, sticking her tongue out a little with concentration as she negotiated the belt buckle. Then she unzipped my fly and slowly pulled them down, exposing my panties which was doing a poor job of containing my new member, which strained against the fabric. I stepped out of my shorts and kicked them aside.

Delicately, she pulled my panties out and over my new cock, so as not to snag it as she pulled them down. As she bent further down my dick actually poked her in the ear, and we both laughed. I kicked my panties away, and she gently grabbed my cock by the base of the shaft and leaned forward to kiss the tip. Looking up at me with those big baleful eyes she then flickered her tongue over its prick.

Her tongue looked both warm and cool at the same time, and I longed to experience their sensation on the other parts of my body.

Soon she put the whole prick in her mouth, kissing it and pulling back so it literally popped out of her mouth each time. And what a wonderful popping noise she made.

She was a pro, I'll give her that. I barely managed to keep me cumming too soon, much to my delight.

She took more of the cock into her mouth, each sucking movement brought her further and further down its length. I didn't think she would take the whole stiff rod, but she did. It was literally hitting the back of her throat! Over and over she managed this until she withdrew it entirely to get a gasp of unobstructed air. My new cock was slick with her saliva, and one thick string of it extended from the tip of its prick all the way to her bottom lip.

She noticed and snagged it with her tongue and slurped it up like spaghetti, following it until she was on my dick again. She played her spit covered lips over its prick until it glistened.

Real or not, it took everything I had not to blow my load right then and there.

Instead, I eased her back onto the bed, hooked a finger into her g-string and slid it off. Her pussy was amazing, like a fleshy clam, with a trim and well groomed thatch of hair about it. Almost like an arrow pointing down! Not sure if that was intentional or not but I sure as hell didn't need directions. Her ass cheeks poked out a little emphasizing her clean little ass hole.

I'd attend to that pleasure spot later. But first, some hardcore fucking!

She quickly reached back and grabbed a condom pack. She had the wrapper open and a condom sliding onto my cock in no time flat!

Gotta love a pro.

Then she took that bottle of lubricant and squirted a good amount in her hand. Then she she rubbed it on my dick, then used the last by rubbing it slowly onto her pussy. She smiled seductively at me. I didn't need any more encouragement.

With my slicker rod at the ready I spread her legs, pushing her knees almost up by her ears. Her gorgeous little pussy begged to be violated and violated hard. So, without any guidance of hands, I moved my hips forward and pointed my cock until it was on the mark. I eased up and the tip easily slid into her. She made a slight show of gasping, but I knew from past experience that this wasn't where the fun really began.

I slide easily into her, pinning her against the mattress. I wiggled my legs up more so my knees were on either side of her hips, and I started to fuck her. Back and forth, back and forth. In and out, in and out. I enjoyed watching the play of her flesh yielding to my stiff cock as I worked her pussy. She was well trimmed, closely shaved actually, and I had a very good close of view of her moist flesh.

I managed this for quite a while. I'm not the most fit girl. But I can give'er as good as the futa swinging gal. And Nah didn't seem to care in the least that I didn't have the body of a super model. A random tryst was just for the fun, regardless of what each participant looks like. Or magical changes that took place.

Soon I was gasping for air from the effort, my legs ached, and my abdominal muscles (I'm sure I had some under that little belly somewhere) began to burn. But I kept going. I was determined to fuck the hell out of her.

At some point she tapped my arm, indicating she wanted to stop. Reluctantly I did. Well, maybe I was a little relieved but I wasn't going to tell her that. She pushed me back by my hips until my dick slid out of her. Then she shoved me backwards into a laying position. I thought she was going to mount me, but, instead I was surprised.

She spun around, squatting above me, and for a few glorious moments, her firm, gum-drop shaped ass pressed into my face. All the while she played with my new balls, massaging, and rubbing them. My grin happily disappeared between two insanely firm butt cheeks. I kissed, and gently bit them. Her asshole, clean and definitely an 'innie' brushed the tip of my nose.

Impulsively, I flicked my tongue over it. Nah giggled, and, encouraged by her reaction, did it again. She shuddered, and held her breath in what I took as pleasant surprise. My flicks gradually progressed to full on licking; long, slow and purposeful. Eventually her asshole gleamed with spit.

It felt great knowing I would soon have my cock inside it, pounding away.

I couldn't wait, I flipped her on her side, positioned myself behind her and began massaging her asshole with my fingers. She got the point and grinned over her shoulder at me. She reached between her legs and guided my dick to her. Slowly, she eased its prick into her little brown star, gasping. Again, she added more lubricant. Then I started to slowly work my length into her ass. So slow it was almost glacier like in movement. But it worked. Eventually, I was almost entirely in her, and she was a little looser so I could start moving it in and out. She was braced up on on elbow, grabbing my right butt cheek with her other hand. I kept her leg up by hooking my hand under her knee and propping her legs open. Easier access that way. She gasped, gritted her teeth, and occasionally grabbed my hip to indicate I should slow down.

Her shit was tight, in a manner of speaking.

I worked her like that for as long as she would let me. And believe me when I say I could have fucked her in the ass like that all damn night as I know women who allow it know exactly how good it feels. God knows I did!

When she could no longer handle more, she eased my throbbing member out of her ass, pushing slowly against my hip. After I popped out, she quickly removed the condom. She grabbed another package and giggled wickedly.

I liked this girl's thinking.

We moved things over to the only chair in the room; it was reclined, low to the ground and, conveniently, did not have arms. She pulled me over from the bed to the chair by my dick, then gently shoved me into it.

She then stood over me, legs on either side, her tiny thatch of pubic hair just inches from my face. She opened the condom package, all the while grinning. I stroked my new cock as I waited, and gingerly massaged her clit with the thumb of my other hand, and delighted in the moist sounds it made.

She threw the empty packed away with a flourish, took my thumb from her clit and sucked on it briefly. Then she bent over enough to kiss the tip of my prick. She did this repeatedly, kiss-kiss-kiss, and finished by expertly sheathing my cock with the condom.

Nah grabbed my cock and massaging it over her pussy lips. She made a playful gasping sound, pressing it playfully between her twat's fleshy folds, back and forth, back and forth. Making circular motions with it until this handling made me moan.

With a final laugh, she sudden squatted down over me, jamming my dick inside her almost half way. I shuddered with the quick motion. She then put her hands onto my shoulders for balance, and slowly gyrated her hips in small circles as she slid down my length.

It looked nothing short of wonderful!

Then she settled onto me, with the last bit of my cock neatly locking into her wet yielding flesh. She grabbed my face with both hands and tilted my head back and started to kiss my neck with gusto. Up and down my neck she worked, until I was certain I would have a constellation of hickeys for days to come. (Thank God!) I would wear them like badges of pride.

I took this opportunity to grab her tits (and who wouldn't?). They were quite firm and perky and I kneaded them like balls of dough, playing my thumbs over her pink nipples. I rubbed them round and round, then alternated to stroke there length and occasionally pinched the tips of them, causing her to moan.

She braced her feet on the floor, and began to hop up and down in my lap. The friction her tight wet pussy made wonderful wet noises. I held onto her waist and helped guide the motion. The smack-smack-smack sound of our flesh smacking together was arousing. I leaned back a bit, and enjoyed the up and down shaking of her pert tits. Her mouth was open as she gasped continuously for air.

She then alternated to grinding her hips. Slow at first, until she hit a really good rhythm then she sped it up. I could actually feel my cock knock back and forth inside her. Wow!

At one point, I almost came. I tilted my head back, moaning loudly and roughly squeezed her tits. She immediately stopped, gave me a kiss on the chin, saying 'No, no, no! Not yet for you." She waited patiently for me to return from the brink, and only then did she resume her grinding. No cumming just yet!

A good long while later, I surprised her by snaking a hand around her back and pressing her firmly against my chest. Then I stood up, hanging onto the chair for balance (hey, I'm not as young as I use to be) and waddled over to the bed, where I eased her down. Bracing her feet against my shoulders, I could see her pussy was dripping wet from all the vigorous work I had given it.

Then, like a real trooper, I slide back inside her. This time I really gave it to her; the full length out, and then slammed the entire thing back in causing my new dangling balls to smack hard against her little asshole. Again and again and again. Even in her compact position she looked amazing, her tits jiggle around wildly with my hard pounding.

I pounded that pussy for as long as I could. You could say I tapped that until I couldn't tap anymore!

It was time. The feeling rushed up on me suddenly and I had to let it out. Gotta let the role-playing take control. The greatest feeling!

I pulled out of her with a wet slick sound and quickly positioned myself next to her head, my cock aimed at her head. With a clumsy effort, I managed to yank off the condom, and tossed it against the wall where it stuck. But I didn't care, I had a face to defile!

Vigorously stroking it, favouring her face to heighten the sensation, I squeezed my dick hard. I gritted my teeth, lost in the moment's intensity. I opened my eyes and saw Nah looking up at me from beneath my cock, smiling with expectation.

That was all it took.

I *exploded* with a loud cry of pleasure. With my swollen prick aimed right at her face, a huge load splattered all over her. Gobs of cum spurted out in pulsing succession. Thick white rivulets cascading off her check, across her nose (and I got some inside a nostril). One squirt landed over her left eye and made one of mark across her forehead like that Nike logo.

I looked down at her in triumph. Fuck she looked sexy with her face slathered with my magical man seed. But I noticed I had completely missed one important part.

I held her head down with one hand and leaned in closer with my cock. I indicated she should pucker her lips which she complied with a giggle. I then smacked my dick against her lips. Smack – Smack – Smack, until the last of what was in it had glossed her beautiful lips, and even dribbled a little down her chin to make a small pool in the hollow of her throat.

That was it for me. I collapsed onto the bed next to her. I was out for the count.

She cuddled against me, our sweat mingling and I started to feel that pleasant soreness begin to seep through my abs and butt. I worked them hard!

I could feel the futa-totem throbbing in my asshole.

Soon, almost like any other random girl did, she started to make sounds about having to leave. I gave her a kiss on the forehead and said it was okay.

She leaped out of bed with a girlish squeal of delight, much to my chagrin. How could she still have all that energy? Women.

As I laid back in the bed, naked, spent, magic cock still waving to the room, I watched as she went through her routine of cleaning herself up and getting ready to leave. I hungrily watched her glide around the room, and enjoyed every pleasant jiggle of flesh. Flesh that I got to see, touch, taste and lick in the hour or so before.

If felt liberating. I felt like a woman. Not the ignored creature that I was in my home country, but a real woman of the world, enjoying one of the pleasures that the rest of humanity were able to experience.

God, I love Thailand.

After she got fully dressed and gathered her things, she playfully jumped on the bed and leaned over me. She was so beautiful. And, only a short while ago that stunning face was completely glazed by me!

"You have phone?" she asked. I found it on the nightstand and gave it to her. She then programmed it with her number and gave it back. "You call me, ok?" Why wouldn't I agree?

Then, I got up and without bothering to dress I walked her to the door. She pouted a little but then burst into a giggling fit and hugged me and gave me a peck on the cheek. She slapped my dick playfully. Then she slipped out the door with a smile and then I was alone. I hadn't noticed but I was grinning from ear to ear.

One down, many more to go. And now I was hungry. Time to eat and restore those well spent calories.

Dinner tastes so much better after cumming all over the face of a Thai beauty.

After I finished eating, I would get down to business of finding yet another good, preferably all night-long, girl. The futa-totem would be well used this trip.

Hey, now wouldn't this look enticing on a travelling brochure:

'Cum To Thailand!'

END

# Her Big Surprise (Futa-Totem)

"I've had it with cheating women!" cried Marla into her cell phone.

Her friend, Kimberly, who was on the receiving end of this declaration, tried to calm her down. "Oh, Marla, honey," she said. "They're not all bad. Some of them are genuinely cowed enough to know they shouldn't mess with alpha females like us."

Neither woman felt such a statement was close to the truth, but it certainly helped Marla a little to think it was. At least for the moment. Was she ready to give up on relationships all together?

Marla paced her apartment living room. "I don't care to find out anymore. So many games, so many lies. A woman can't get anything honest from someone who makes a habit of lying. They just can't be trusted."

She had reason to be angry. Andrea, her girlfriend... ex-girlfriend... had just admitted to her, not fifteen minutes ago, that she had been unfaithful to her for the last two months of their relationship. With some waitress at a bar she frequented.

The coward had told her over the phone, too. Andrea didn't have the nerve, or the guts, to tell Marla to her face. Marla would have liked to have punched her! Or at least scratched her eyes out.

Kimberly continued to try and calm her friend down. "Yeah, they're scum. They can't be trusted. Maybe you should just, I dunno, maybe take a break from serious relationships for a little bit. I know this just happened and all, but maybe this was for the best."

Marla had paced into the bedroom and caught her reflection in the closet mirror. She was still in a bathrobe, having showered in preparation for going out with Andrea that evening, and bring her back for a very big Futa surprise. She gave her body an appraising once over. She was hot dammit! Why would any woman in her right mind even entertain the idea of screwing around behind her back? Especially *this* lovely back! She turned and lifted up the robe exposing a very firm, and pleasantly shaped, tear drop ass.

No more of this honey-dew for her!

"I know, I know," Marla said. "It just hurts. I thought we had something truly meaningful. But I guess it wasn't meaningful enough." She gave her own ass a smack and was pleased that it barely shook. "Maybe I should just pick up some random piece of ass at the bar and screw the hell out of it."

"Yes!" Kimberly shouted. "Nothing better than cheap meaningless sex with a stranger to help you get through times of trouble. Plus, with that little magical device you keep that box wouldn't hurt either."

"Jealous?" asked Marla.

"Yes! Where in the hell did you get a magical dildo from, anyway?"

"Some secrets are meant to stay that way: secret."

"Bitch!"

Marla managed a laugh. Kimberly could always make her feel better. But, right now, she just needed more.

Just then the downstairs buzzer rang.

"Who's that?" asked Kimberly.

"Oh, shoot. I was expecting a package delivered today for work." Andrea had called her right after she got the a call-confirmation, asking if she would be home. She buzzed in whoever it was without answering.

"Wait a second, sister," said Kimberly, conspiratorially. "What if it's a babe?"

Marla scoffed. "No, it's always this little fat woman who smells of sweat and cheese."

"You should *do* her!"

"No way!" Marla shuddered. Just the thought of it made her skin crawl.

"Or, it could be someone different. A moonlighting lingerie model."

Marla's brow furrowed. "Wow, you have quite the imagination. Well, if that were the case, she'd get one hell of a tip outta me, tonight."

"That a girl!" cried Kimberly.

Marla was only half joking. It would take a lot to get her to indulge in a casual quickie with a stranger. But her mind wandered to the little wooden box in the living room...

There was a knock at the door. Marla took a moment to look herself over in the living room mirror. The robe hung half open, so she cinched it closed. It accentuated her voluptuous breasts. Her muscular legs were bare for all to see. The robe only just covered her ass. She hadn't put on any underwear after she finished showering, and there certainly wasn't any time now to put some on.

*I do look damn sexy, though*, she thought to herself. At least miss chubby from the courier place will get a little bit of an eye full.

While she walked to the door, Kimberly was chanting in the phone, "Hot sex! Hot sex! Hot sex!"

Marla could only roll her eyes. *As if.*

She peered through the peek hole.

A tall beautiful woman was standing out there. Holding a boxed package. Her boxed package.

"Uh," was all Marla was able to say.

Kimberly immediately pounced. "What? WHAT?!"

Marla found herself whispering, her eye glued to the hole, drinking in the sweety outside. "It's not the usual chick. She's..." *Vivacious.*

"So? Is she pretty, or just pretty enough?" asked Kimberly, intrigued with her friend's change of tone. "Either will do for now."

Marla realized she had been staring at the woman entirely too long. She took a deep breath and opened the door.

The peephole view did not do this walking Greek Goddess justice. Tall, cute, and perfectly toned, the woman gave Marla a pearly white smile.

"Hi," she said. "I have a package for Marla?"

Marla was momentarily speechless. She was also alarmed to feel a dampness grow between her upper thighs.

"Yeah," Marla managed to stammer smiling, still a little shocked. She stepped back, letting the other woman inside. She closed the door behind her.

Marla had forgotten her cell phone was in her free hand, until she dimly heard Kimberly cry out: "Do her! Screw her brains out! Give her a tip she'll never forget!"

Marla quickly hung up. The delivery girl... woman... hottie, crooked a questioning eyebrow. Marla managed not to blush. "My friend is being annoying," she finally said, and immediately felt ridiculous.

The woman continued smiling politely, "Our delivery service has that effect on folks." Her eyes were an incredible piercing blue, and they glanced down at Marla's robe, and then at her legs before quickly returning to her eyes again.

Marla was surprised to find herself thrilled at this.

"You're not the usual courier lady."

"Oh, you probably get Patricia," her voice was soft, but confident. The kind you wouldn't mind having whispering instructions in your ear. "She called in sick so I had to pick up the slack."

Marla nodded, dully. This girl was a lot to take in. Marla suddenly found herself wondering just how much that would be, and in how many positions. "I've never seen you before. Are you new there?"

"New? Oh, more than that. I'm the owner."

She looked down at the company name on the package. It said Janice's Package Delivery Service. The satchel bag, that was slung over her shoulder, also had these words stencilled on it. "You're Janice?" Marla said, incredulous.

"The big boss lady herself," Janice said with a confident grin.

Marla found she was most definitely horny, now. Maybe there was a package Janice could delivery for her, and not the one in her hands.

She was struck with a strong impulse and felt an overwhelming urge to act on it. Kimberly was right. Meaningless sex with a stranger could be exactly what she needs right now. Especially with this particular beautiful stranger.

"Oh, uh, please bring it in the living room," Marla said, walking away from her. Janice more or less had to follow. As Marla turned she sneaked a look at the other woman's wedding finger. Barren.

Good.

Marla also noted Janice's eyes fell on her butt as she talked to her over her shoulder.

"Right over there, please," she pointed at the big coffee table which was between the couch and the easy chair. There was a plate of warmed up pizza she was nibbling on, sitting on the table. Next to it, was a narrow wooden box.

Janice gave a short nod to her as she passed. Marla inhaled her wake as she did so, and liked the hint of her perfume, and the slight tinge of sweat. Most likely from working hard most of the night.

Marla yearned to make her sweat some more.

Janice placed the package on the table, and as she turned toward her, Marla quickly undid her robes, and let them fall to the floor. She put her hands on her curvy hips and bent a knee slighting for enticing emphasis.

Janice froze, eyes locked on her naked form. Marla was sexy as all hell, and she could see she thought the same.

"Well, Janice of Janice's Delivery Service," she said, with fire in her eyes, and a seductive tone in her voice. "I have a way I can pay you properly for that package."

Janice's jaw dropped, and her eyes roved over Marla. Janice was appropriately shell shocked, and took several moments to compose herself.

Who could blame her?

"I, uh..." Janice stammered.

Deciding to take her initiative even further Marla didn't want Janice to have to decide on her own. She walked forward, breasts jiggling hypnotically, and grabbed at her t-shirt. She only flinched just slightly, as if her brain was only now catching up with unfolding events, but she smiled and yielded.

Janice chuckled, quickly removed her shoulder satchel and placed in on the floor. Then raised her arms so Marla could pull the it off of her.

Her chest did not disappoint. Muscles lined her body and stomach. Bra-less, her breasts were small and perky, and her arms were hard and lean.

Marla ran her hands over Janice's chest, massaging her tits. "You lift a lot of heavy packages to get a body like that?" she asked teasingly.

"Something like that," Janice said. Her hands rubbed Marla's shoulders, and up and down her arms. Then she cupped Marla's ample breasts, squeezing them. Marla found her hands were calloused and strong, but gentle, too. Just the way she liked them.

She grabbed at Janice's belt and undid it with a playful grunt. She smiled and let her work at it. When unbuckled, she unzipped her fly, then squatted down in front of her, pulling her pants down. Marla managed to work them to her hips, and with one final tug, yanked them down to her knees.

Janice's pussy was there, waiting to be licked. Marla rubbed her fingers against it gently. She looked up at Janice's face. "I have something that would add something quite special to the occasion.

Perplexed Janice said, "Ok, what? Whips and chains? I would be into that."

Marla chuckled. "Even better than those. Trust me." She went over to the table, and retrieved the wooden box. She undid the clasp, and opened the lid. The Futa-Totem was cushioned within. Marla angled the box so Janice could see it.

Janice's eyes were wide. "Is... is that what I think it is?"

Surprised, Marla said, "You know what this is?"

"Yes!" Janice said. "My God, I thought I'd never see one again."

"You have?"

"Once before. Used it with a girlfriend of mine. Amazing thing isn't it?"

"You bet it is!" Marla laughed. She gently took the Futa-Totem out of the box, placed the box back onto the table and went to Janice.

"So," Marla said. "Fucker, or Fuckee?"

"Huh?" Janice said.

"The last time you used one of these," Marla said. "Were you the fucker or the 'fuckee'?"

"Ah," Janice said, understanding. "I was the 'fuckee'. I was 'fuckeed' pretty damn hard to." She grinned.

"Well, then," Marla said. "Care to do the honors this time?"

"Yes, ma'am!"

"Okay, then," Marla said, dropping to her knees. "Now, turn around. She me that succulent asshole of yours. I want to get it nice and lubbed up for this." She smiled mischievously.

Happy to oblige, Janice turned around. Her wonderful tear-drop shaped ass presented itself to Marla's face. Marla give it a playful smack. It was so damn firm, it barely moved.

"Nice," Marla said.

"So I've been told," said Janice.

Marla ran her free hand over Janice's butt cheeks, exploring their shape. God damn she liked a great ass, and this girl has one of the better ones she's had the pleasure of getting up close and personal with.

"Bend over just a little," Marla said.

Janice did so.

Marla used her free hand placed it into the crack of Janice's ass and firmly grabbed the rounded underside of an ass cheek. Then she pushed it up and to the side exposing a beautiful little puckered anus.

"Mmmm," Marla said. "This looks very lickable. May I?"

"Oh, please do," said Janice. "It's what it's there for."

Marla leaned forward and wedged her face between Janice's ass cheeks. Their warm, firm flesh slid across the sides of her face up to her ears. She opened her mouth, and stuck out her tongue.

The first lick caused Janice to take a sudden intake of breath. *People are never prepared for the first one,* Marla thought pleasantly.

Then, she licked again. All the way from Janice's taint, then up over the puckered contours of her asshole. Nice and slow. Nice and wet. Again and again.

Janice's mouth was open in pleasant ecstasy, occasionally moaning with a more stronger lick.

For several delightful minutes, Marla licked Janice's asshole. Over and over.

Content with a job well done, she gave it one last lick and leaned back. She presented the Futa-Totem in her other hand.

"Ready?" she asked.

"Ready and willing," said Janice.

"That is what I like to hear!" said Marla.

She gripped the little pink dildo shaped Futa-Totem by its wide base. Marla then gave its tip a good spit. "For good measure," she said.

Then, she teased the tip of the totem into the waiting anus of Janice. It met little resistance. Slowly, she slid it all the way in. Nice and smooth. Janice gave a gasp, but didn't protest. All that was left of the pink Futa-Totem was its fat base, the rest was buried inside Janice's ass.

Happy, Marla said, "Okay, turn around. Now for the cool part."

Janice did. Marla put her hands on the side of Janice's hips holding her steady. Marla and Janice were watching the well shaved portion of Janice's groin, right about the top end of her pussy.

"Feel anything, yet?" asked Marla.

"No, not yet.... OH!" Janice suddenly cried.

Then, right at the spot they were watching, a bump appeared. A large bump. Like something was inside, trying to push its way out.

Just then, the skin that made up the bump formed into a fat prick.

"Oh, my God!" said Janice, awestruck.

The prick moved forward, extending outwards from her flesh. Behind it, exposing itself inch by inch, was the shaft of a cock. As it continued to elongate it became apparent that it was quite large.

"Well, damn!" said Marla as it kept growing. So much so she had to lean back a bit to give it room.

Soon, it stopped. A massive cock now protruded out from Janice's flesh, directly above her pussy.

Janice stared at it, stunned. "It's a monster!"

Marla nodded, "The size is different for each person. No two are really the same." She eyed the horse cock with appreciation. "Looks like you have been blessed in that department."

Suddenly, a sack of skin ballooned outward from under her new shaft, right at the base. It formed itself into a nut sack. First one, then two, testicles practically popped into existence inside it. Her new ball sack dangled provocatively.

Janice tore her gaze from her new monster dick and balls, and looked at Marla eagerly. "I wanna fuck you with it!" she said, grabbing her new piece of meat, shaking it. "Fuck you *really* hard!"

"That sounds like a great plan to me!" Marla said. "Now lets get these pants off." She tugged at Janice's pants, which were still around her knees, hard.

The sudden motion of the pants had caused Janice to lose her grip on her new dick, and it swung around and hit Marla on the side of the nose.

"Oh, my God!" She gasped. Janice smiled down at her. Marla blinked in surprise. "You know, I don't remember expecting this kind of package at all," She giggled, amazed.

"It's an extra service. For hot, sexy customers only," Janice said.

Marla pulled off Janice's shoes, and then aided her in removing the pants from her ankles. Marla then turned her attention to the large erect cock in front of her, which demanded attention.

Grabbing it eagerly, Marla stroking it up and down, marvelling at its thickness, and heft. Stealing her courage, Marla then put it in her mouth, and started to suck. It was large, but she had managed this size dick before.

Janice sighed with the sudden feel of Marla's warm wet mouth on her new fat prick, and the motion of her lips moving up and down her shaft. Because of its size, the sound of Marla's slurping and occasional gagging was more prominent.

Up and down Marla worked it. Long minutes of concentrated effort, with her mouth made the dick glisten with her spit, creating a slight foam at its base. Some spit eventually dribbled down to Janice's balls to dangle there in an elastic string.

Satisfied she had properly welcomed Janice into her home, she leaned back a bit for a breather, and gasped.

Marla motioned to the easy chair, "Sit down. I have an idea."

"I like your ideas so far," Janice said with wide appreciative eyes. She did as she was told.

Marla turned to the still-hot pizza slice on the table and stuck her fingers in it. As she tried to pick at a ring of green pepper she squealed girlishly from its heat. Finding one that suited her needs, she turned towards Janice, and the other woman's eyes widened at what Marla had in mind.

Gingerly, she broke it at one point, then wrapped the green pepper around the base of the thick cock. Because she was so well shaved Janice hissed slightly, but not with great pain.

"You okay?" Marla asked coyly.

"Oh, yeah," Janice said through gritted teeth. "I knew my customers were hot but not *this* hot."

Marla grinned up at her, then swirled her tongue around the swollen prick. She took it in her mouth, and slowly worked her way down its length, occasionally pausing to wiggle her head back and forth to help it past the hook at the back of her throat. Janice gasped, amazed. Marla's tongue poked out of the bottom of her gaping mouth. The cock's girth had forced her mouth wide, stretching her lips around it. Spittle gathered in sticky strands at the corners.

With amazing patience, Marla neither gagged, or pulled back. She gazed up at Janice with big eyes, and her tongue prodded the green pepper until she managed to catch it. Then, very slowly, she slid back up the entire shaft, green pepper in tow.

Sucking it off the tip, the green pepper dangled from her mouth. Then Marla leaned back, plucking it in her fingers and smiling at Janice triumphantly.

"Impressive!" Janice said, laughing. "My turn to do a trick."

Janice eased Marla up off her knees, and had her sit in the easy chair this time. Marla spread her legs by hooking her knees over the arms, exposing her very well shaved, and *very* wet pussy to the other woman. She rubbed at her clit playfully.

"Do as you please, delivery girl," she said while teething the tip of one of her fingers.

"Oh, I will," Janice returned. With one finger she dipped into the tomato sauce of the pizza slice. Careful to get enough, she then slowly spread it around Marla's pussy, smearing it completely with sauce.

It was Marla's turn to grit her teeth from the heat, as Janice worked her fingers around her clit. Then Janice leaned forward, and with her hands firmly holding Marla's legs wide at the thighs, she started to lick.

Up and down, then all around, Janice licked and slurped. When a little sauce dripped down into the slight hollow at Marla's asshole, she slurped it up. Janice then stayed there, rimming her asshole with her tongue.

Marla gasped with pleasure, squeezing her tits, pinching at their erect nipples.

Then Janice returned her attention to Marla's pussy, taking long deliberate licks, making sure she wasn't finished until it was completely cleaned of tomato sauce.

Janice grinned up at her and said, "Tomato sauce never tasted so damn good."

She smiled back and said, "Glad to finally be on the menu."

Janice then stood, giant cock still hard and ready. She leaned forward so she was hovering over Marla, and pointed her massive dick downward as far as it would go. She stuck its prick into Marla's waiting pussy. Marla gasped, and grabbed onto Janice's hips. Janice paused, and said, "I have a very big package to give you, ma'am. Are you ready for it?"

"Yes! Yes I am!" Marla declared.

And with that, Janice suddenly slammed the entire length of her long cock deep inside her. Marla gasped with the hard penetration. Janice then lifted her ass up again, so the entire length of the dick was nearly unsheathed from Marla, and slammed it down again.

Over and over she did this, getting faster and faster. Marla moaned with each pelvic thrust. Long wonderful minutes passed as she slammed Marla's pussy again and again. Eventually, the intensity got to be so much Marla's eyes rolled upwards showing only their whites.

Janice reached around Marla's neck and pulled against her head slightly, so as to cut off some of the circulation. She gasped for air while Janice continued her relentless hammering. She eased off her head only when she seemed close to passing out.

Then Janice slowed, making easy gyrating motions with her hips. Janice wanted to give her a little time to recover before giving her what was about to happen next.

When Marla seemed okay, Janice slipped out of her, and her pussy gave a wet fart. Janice then turned Marla around and pushed her on the chair so her upper body leaning over the back of it. Marla's beautiful tits hung down over the back edge. Janice perched behind her, and smacked her incredible ass. It shook only slightly, being so firm.

Then Janice eased her dick into Marla's pussy again, which was now sopping wet. Making sure Marla was firmly pressed up against the chair, hands holding her hips tightly, Janice began to pump back and forth. Each time she slammed her ass Marla grunted with the force of it. Janice could sense the bottom of the massive cock rub hard against the inside of her and Janice knew she felt it, too.

Again, Janice was relentless in her pounding. Over and over. Marla gasped and moaned and dug her fingers into the chair. She was almost certain Janice was going to pound her straight through it.

The apartment filled with the ceaseless smacking of flesh on flesh. Punctuated with their moans of pleasure.

Eventually, Janice grabbed Marla's arms, and pulled them back by the elbows, forcing her to arch her back. Her long blond hair dangled down to almost brush against the small of her back, and shook with each hard thrust. Janice began to slam against her even harder and Marla moaned more deeply.

On the other side of the living room was a mirror. In the reflection, Janice could see Marla's firm breasts moving with the harsh pounding rhythm. Her mouth was open, eyes were closed, and her brow was furrowed with gritting pleasure.

Over and over; again and again Janice tapped that ass, until she could see that Marla was getting red where their flesh smacked against one an other.

Janice, keeping with her role, could not keep up this relentless pace. With both the feeling of Janice rubbing wetly inside her, and seeing Marla's wonderfully firm flesh vibrating with her effort, Janice felt she was about to explode.

"I'm gonna cum!" Janice practically shouted.

Quickly, Marla pulled her body forward so as to unsheathe the cock from her, and she spun around. Janice stood, stroking her dick vigorously. Marla placed the bottom of her open mouth against the base of its prick. Her tongue tickled at it eagerly, and her eyes stared up at Janice with hunger.

Janice stroked faster, and then exploded with a loud moan. The hot cum spat out all over Marla; many hot squirts went into her mouth which slid down her tongue and pooled at the back of her throat. Over her face in long sticky strands that splayed across her cheeks and forehead. In the corner of one eye, down her chin, and he even got some in her blond hair.

As Janice sagged with completion, Marla made a dramatic show of swallowing.

She smacked her mouth, and rolled her tongue around her lips, getting every white bit. A long thick strand still hung from her chin as she grinned widely at Janice.

"Mmmm," Marla said. "Delicious!"

Marla then grabbed Janice's cock again, and sucked it, nursing the last of its load. She wanted every little bit of it.

It was while Marla was doing this, and looking up at the exhausted pleasure in Janice's face, that she made a wondrous conclusion:

She needed to get courier service more often, dammit!

END

# Also by Danii Dezire

Adults Only
Best Friends
Martin & Cindy
New Lovers
Pam & Roger
Sandy & Hank
Tim & Angie
X-Rated
Chocolate Milk
Freaky Futa
Futa Rama
Have Futa, Will Travel
Her Big Surprise
Red & Raw
Rough & Raw
Spanked Raw
The Gender Swap Device
Wet & Raw
Being Bad: Part One
Futa Totem Collection #1
Going Raw, The Collection